BADLANDS

Jason Nickey

UNCOMFORTABLY DARK HORROR

Book Cover Design and wrap by Christy Aldridge of Grim Poppy Design

First edition 2025

Edited & formatted by 360 Editing, a division of Uncomfortably Dark Horror.

Editors: Candace Nola & Mort Stone

Published by Uncomfortably Dark Horror, owned and operated by Candace Nola. Pittsburgh, PA

Follow us on all social media, our Patreon, or on our website to stay up to date on new releases, appearances, and more!

Committed to *"bringing you the best in horror, one uncomfortably dark page at a time."*

*Patreon*www.patreon.com/c/u12231330

*Website*www.uncomfortablydark.com

ALSO BY JASON NICKEY

NOVELLAS
Wreckage
Jasper And The Appalachian Zombies
Road Hazards
Don't Look In The Trees
Rural Decay
Past Due: Rural Decay 2

COLLECTIONS
Static And Other Stories
They Come From Within
Slush Pile
Channels

"BADLANDS is not your typical horror read, all flashy or full of jump scares- it's a slow, character -driven horror story that builds its tension from real emotion and guilt. It weaves a tale of old friendships and love, all to be rekindled for a trip in the desert that you will not see coming."—Dan Shrader, author of CABIN BLACK

"How can something be so unflinching, yet surprisingly tender? Jason Nickey doesn't pull any punches. BADLANDS is pure menace in the desert. Incredibly sharp, sunburnt, and soaked in blood."—Cassan dra Celia, author of HOUSE OF HARROW

"Jason Nickey delivers a vision quest into hell with the BADLANDS. The story grips you from the beginning daring you to venture further into the dark."—Matthew Lutton, author of THE MORNINGSTAR CONFESSION

"BADLANDS is an absolute bombshell on top of an already untouchable backlog of great writing by Jason Nickey. His great-

ness never ceases to amaze me!"—Stuart Bray, author of BLADE IN THE BATH

"A cautionary tale that will leave your stomach in knots."—Patrick Tumblety, author of ONE FRIGHT ONLY

CONTENTS

DEDICATION

For Jared, my partner in life, crime, and travel.

Chapter 1

I STEPPED OUT OF the office building after a long day at work and took in the lush shades of green on the surrounding trees. It was a bit cooler than normal for mid-July and was a nice break from the heat wave we'd been experiencing for a few weeks. For a moment, it distracted me from the night ahead. It was my tiny respite from the anxiety that had been plaguing me all day.

It was a Thursday, and I had taken the following day off. I had plans with some old friends to fly out to New Mexico the following day for what was described to me as a 'mystery adventure'.

On the surface, it sounded like a fun getaway; however, it was the company I would be keeping that had me anxious.

Troy Grishaber, an old friend of mine from high school, had set up the trip. It was meant as a reunion for the crew of friends we had throughout middle and high school. The crew, jokingly referred to by many as the fantastic four, consisted of me, Troy, Marcus Greenhall, and Levi Granger.

We met in sixth-grade and remained close friends from then on. There wasn't much we didn't do as a group. Most of our classmates, along with the people in town, figured we would remain that way for the rest of our lives. It didn't quite work out that way, though. Like many friend groups, we slowly lost touch in the years that followed.

The weekend getaway was to be the first time all four of us had been together in twenty years. The mere thought of it gave me anxiety. Not that I held any ill will towards any of them, but they've all been far more successful in life than I have.

Marcus ended up becoming a lawyer, recently making partner at a new firm. Levi got his logistics degree and started his own construction company. Troy, however, was the one that really outshone our group. He got into college on a football scholarship, and it only went uphill from there. He ended up playing professionally for fifteen years. He retired shortly before planning the trip.

As for me, sports and school were never my strong suit. I attended community college for a few semesters but ended up dropping out. Since then, I've spent my time bouncing around from one dead-end job to another. Needless to say, I wasn't looking forward to the "So, how's life going?" portion of the weekend's small talk.

What added to my anxiety was not only the fact that Levi would be there, but that he was supposed to be driving to my place that night so we could fly out together in the morning.

There was history between me and Levi; history I had been dwelling on for far too long. To say I had a crush on him throughout our friendship would be an understatement. In truth, by the time we finished high school, I was in love with him. My feelings for him advanced to that level during our senior year, right after we hooked up for the first time. Afterwards, we hooked up on a regular basis, jumping at any chance we could get to be alone, which was limited to the times when nobody would find out.

While I was on my way to being ready to come out, Levi was not; nor would he ever be. He got married shortly after graduating from college and had two teenage sons who were now in high school. Even after twenty years, I still felt a stab in my heart any time he posted a picture of his happy family on social media. He'd been able to do the one thing I hadn't; move on from what we had together.

I had spent the last twenty years jumping back and forth in relationships that were doomed before they started. I felt pathetic most of the time, and I was terrified to see him tonight, terrified of what emotions seeing him would stir up. Especially since I basically became a recluse after my ex died two years ago. Levi was the only one to come to the funeral, which honestly just made the whole situation harder.

A part of me dreaded this impromptu reunion, but I also didn't want to be the only one to not show up. I still cared about these guys enough to put on a happy face and do my best to enjoy myself.

Chapter 2

I SPENT THE ENTIRE drive home with an overwhelming knot forming in my gut. All I could think about was the bottle of vodka in my freezer. It felt as though it was calling my name. I ended up pouring a drink as soon as I walked through the door of my apartment.

As I sipped on my drink, I knew I still had packing to do, but I scoured my fridge for a bite to eat first. I ended up settling on a slice of leftover pizza from the night before. It was something that had become a fairly common dinner for me in recent years.

As I chewed on the pizza, which was a little tougher than I would have preferred, I realized that I had ordered it two nights before. *Jesus*, I thought, *I'm living like a divorced dad.* I felt like a loser. Here, the guy I've been in love with since I was a teenager was coming to visit, and he would find me living like a fucking slob. I knew I would have to order takeout or something once he got here. I didn't really have the money to do so, especially with the possible expenses the upcoming trip would bring, but I knew I had to do something.

I sighed before throwing the crust in the trash and making my way to the bedroom to finish packing my things for the weekend. I had only grabbed a few things out of my drawers before realizing that most of my clean clothes were still sitting in the dryer. I turned to head to my washer and dryer in the hallway and scoffed at the pile of dirty clothes piled up in the corner of my room. *Divorced dad or teenager?* I thought with a laugh.

I had just finished folding my clean clothes and packing when I heard a knock at the door. My heart began racing, knowing it was Levi. My legs felt like Jell-O, and my body shook as I made my way to the door.

I opened the door to find Levi standing there. He arrived earlier than expected, and I was taken aback by how good he looked in person. It had only been two years since I had last seen him, but the pictures on his social media had never done him justice. Seeing him always took me by surprise. I stood there dumbfounded.

"Well. You gonna invite me in?" he asked with a goofy smile on his face. A smile I hadn't realized I missed so much until that moment.

"Oh, yeah. Sorry. Just can't believe it's been so long."

"Sorry, my ass. Bring it in, motherfucker," he said as he pulled me in for a hug. I felt as though I were melting.

He stepped back after the hug that lasted just slightly too long and looked around. "Nice place."

I scoffed, "Yeah, sure. For a shoebox."

I tried to ease the sarcasm in my tone. I knew he was just being polite.

"Really good to see you, Jimmy. It's been too long," he said.

"You too, Levi. You too."

"Not to be rude, but where's your bathroom? I've been holding in this piss for an hour."

I laughed and gestured for him to follow me. We stepped into my bedroom, and I pointed to the door in the far corner. "Just through there." I blushed from embarrassment, hoping he wasn't disgusted by how cluttered my place was.

"Thanks, man," he said before running to the bathroom.

While he was pissing, I zipped my suitcase and set it on the floor. I waited there for him to finish, unsure of what to say next.

"Hope I'm not too early, man," he said as he emerged from the bathroom. "I left early hoping I could beat traffic." He began unbuttoning his shirt as he continued, "I still hit some on my way out though, but it wasn't too bad."

I stood there and listened as he kicked his shoes off and began unbuttoning his pants. I was so confused that I had no idea what to say.

"It was a pretty smooth drive after that. Gives us more time to hang out without the others around."

By this point, he was fully naked. He stood there, staring at me before speaking up once more. "Do... uh... you not wanna?" he asked with a confused look.

"Huh?" I responded.

He approached me and grabbed me by the back of my head, pulling me in for a kiss. We stayed like that for a moment before he pulled away. "Fuck," he said with a sigh, "It's been way too goddamn long."

He must have seen the look of shock on my face.

"I figured we could... you know," he said, reaching down with his free hand to grab my cock through my pants, "for old time's sake. If it's cool with you."

Feeling the erection growing in my pants, he gave me a devious smile. "I figured you would be down. Get those clothes off."

I sighed, disappointed in myself for letting my libido take over. By the time I had my clothes off, he was bent over in front of me. I hated knowing this was just a fun fling for him, despite it being a lot more for me, but in that moment, I was too weak to say no.

I spat on my hand and shoved my cock in his ass. It went in with ease and made me wonder if he'd been hooking up with other guys on the down-low throughout his marriage. I was a little jealous at the thought but worked through it by taking a few years of sexual frustration out on him.

He didn't seem to mind.

WE LAY THERE IN my bed afterwards, still unclothed. Me hating myself for giving in to the temptation, and him oblivious while smoking a joint. I looked over at him and envied the fact that he was in even better shape than he had been in high school. Toned stomach, muscular arms and legs. I felt very self-conscious as I looked back down at my own body. I wasn't necessarily fat, but despite not having kids, I seemed to have the dad bod thing going on.

I reached over and ran my hand across his stomach. "You've certainly kept yourself in good shape over the years."

"Yeah," he said with a strained voice. He was holding in the smoke. He continued as he finally exhaled, "Go to the gym every day. Gives me a break from the wife and kids."

There it was again. That stabbing feeling. I knew this was just a small sample of what I would be feeling throughout this trip.

"I probably need to start doing the same," I said, hoping to sway the conversation.

"I mean, if you want to. I think you look good though."

I felt myself blushing a bit before grabbing my belly. "Wouldn't mind losing this."

"No way, man," he replied, reaching over to grab my belly himself. "It's hot. Besides, dad bods are in now. Chicks seem to dig it; I'm sure guys do too. I do."

He winked before leaning in and kissing me.

"You ready for this 'mystery adventure'?" I asked, holding up air-quotes.

"Yeah. What the fuck is this all about anyway?" Levi asked. "Did he give you any details?"

I shrugged. I truly had no idea. Troy had sent out an email invite just a week before, referring to it as his retirement party, along with telling us it was a surprise mystery adventure.

It seemed a bit odd when I got the email, especially since it was such short notice. A part of me wanted to decline, but considering he was paying for everyone's airfare, I felt some obligation to go. I had enough vacation time saved up, so it wasn't a big deal to take off, and there was a part of me that wanted to see the guys again.

And I can't deny that Levi, being next to me in my bed, felt good.

————

WE SPENT THE NEXT two hours going back and forth between small talk and fooling around for a while before finally deciding to get off one last time and calling it a night.

When I finally leaned over to turn the light off, he made his way closer to me, wrapping his arm around me and laying his head on my chest. "I've really missed you, Jimmy. I wish you'd come visit me once in a while," he said, his tone serious for the first time that night.

"It's complicated. Let's just enjoy the weekend."

He replied by squeezing me a bit tighter for a moment.

It was just like a repeat of high school. When we were alone, it was like the best relationship anyone could ask for, full of passion and affection. Then, when we weren't alone, it was like bro-mode. Best buddies who carried on and gave each other a hard time. I always struggled with the transition, but he seemed to do it with ease. It always amazed me how he was able to turn it on and off so easily.

That night, with him beside me, I slept better than I had in years. While I knew it was self-destructive, I secretly hoped we would have a room to ourselves at the hotel in New Mexico. It would at least make the time out there a little easier, even if it would destroy me for a while afterwards.

CHAPTER 3

WE WOKE UP FAIRLY early the next morning; however; we didn't exactly get an early start on our drive. We showered, fucked once more, then showered again before finally getting dressed and heading out the door. We took his car since it was newer, but I drove. We stopped for breakfast at a diner on the way out of town. I felt a bit more relaxed as we sat there and ate our food.

Somehow, I seemed to have gotten a little better at accepting the situation ahead of me overnight. I was letting myself just enjoy spending time with Levi again. It almost felt as though no time had passed at all since we had last seen each other. It's strange how that can happen with old friends.

We hit the road as soon as we finished breakfast, and I soon found out that my statement the night before had bothered Levi in some way. We were about fifteen minutes into the drive to the airport when he broke the silence by asking, "So what did you mean last night, when you said, 'It's complicated'?"

There was that knot again. Back in an instant.

"I don't really want to talk about it, Levi. And you probably don't want to hear the real reason anyway."

This seemed to upset him, and his tone turned defensive. "What's that supposed to mean? I'm not the one who's been distant for so long. I'm not the one who can't be bothered to come visit. Hell, I would have come to see you if you had invited me. I mentioned it multiple times, but you never took me up on it. Did I do something to piss you off?"

I sighed. "No... well, kinda. I don't know. It's not that simple."

"We've got an hour drive ahead of us, Jimmy. I've got time. Tell me what it is that's so complicated about visiting each other."

Something inside me snapped, and I decided not to hold back any longer. "Are you that dense, Levi? Are you blind to the fact that I was in love with you back then? Can you not even see that I still am?"

I paused, taking a breath before continuing. Levi sat there in silence.

"You moved on, Levi. Nice house, beautiful wife, happy family. I'm not mad at you for that, but goddamn. Did it never occur to you that it was hard for me to see you with someone else? Did you think I could come to your house and see you with your family and not be at least a little jealous? You had to have known how I felt. I mean, Jesus... I've been with other guys over the years, but they all had one big flaw in common."

He looked at me with concern. "What? Did they hurt you?"

"No... well, yeah, but that's not what I mean. They were all doomed from the start because they couldn't compare to you."

We sat there in silence for a few minutes before I spoke up again. "Look. I know that's not your fault. I know it's not normal to be hung up on somebody for this fucking long. I don't know how to explain it, but it's just how it is. Last night was amazing, but this weekend is going to kill me because when it's over, you'll go back to your family, and I'll go back to being alone. That's why I haven't come to visit. That's why I haven't asked you to come up."

"I..." he began, pausing for a moment as if he was about to cry, "I'm sorry. You know I've always had feelings for you too, Jimmy. That's just not the life I want to live."

"If that's the only reason, then you're a coward, Levi."

"Maybe I am. I'm not denying that, but I've done the best I could with my life. I'm sorry if that's kept you from doing the same."

"Sometimes... sometimes I wonder if it would be this way if our first time together hadn't been *that* night."

He flinched at this statement, at my emphasis on 'that.' "Don't bring that up, Jimmy. Our friendship, the four of us... It's been surrounded by some pretty messed up shit. We've all worked hard to move past it."

"Well, sometimes it feels like you've all moved past me too."

———

THE NIGHT I WAS referring to — the night that Levi and I were intimate with each other for the first time — was a night that would taint the four of us for the rest of our lives.

It was early in our senior year. There was a party that night, and I spent most of the day over at Levi's house helping him do yardwork. While working, I kept taking glances at Levi. He already had his shirt off, and the sweat glistening on his skin sent my hormones into overdrive. I could swear I noticed him taking similar glances at me, but I figured it was just my imagination. I had been crushing on him since the moment we met and figured there was absolutely zero chance of the feeling being reciprocated.

By the time we had finished, we were covered in sweat, dirt, and lawn clippings. We both felt disgusting, so we decided to shower before meeting up with Marcus and Troy.

Before grabbing a towel, I asked Levi if I could use his parents' shower since they weren't home. It was more like a room than a shower, with dual showerheads and plenty of room for two people. I had seen it before when I had visited and had always wanted to use it.

He nodded and followed me in with two towels before stepping out of the room.

I had just gotten the water to the right temperature and stepped underneath when I was startled by the sound of the shower door opening. I turned to see Levi standing there completely naked as he entered the shower and turned on the water for the second shower-head.

I immediately began shaking, my teenage hormones taking over at being naked together.

He didn't say anything as he began lathering up. Within a few minutes, glances were exchanged, and erections began to form. Before I knew it, we were all over each other like rabid animals. We barely even toweled off before climbing into his parents' bed and finishing what we started in the shower.

We lay there for a while in each other's arms after we had finished up, neither of us saying a word other than Levi whispering, "Why don't you stay here tonight after the party."

I responded by holding his body against mine a little tighter.

Before too long, the phone rang, interrupting our peaceful embrace. I watched in awe as Levi stood up and left the room to answer it, feeling like this whole day had just been a dream.

He returned to the room a few minutes later. It had apparently been Troy on the phone, asking when we were heading over. Knowing we had to get moving, we both hopped in the shower once more to rinse off before getting dressed. We barely said a word to each other as we headed out to Troy's house. Once there, we hopped in the back seat of Troy's car and the four of us drove out to a bonfire party that some of our classmates were holding at a lake just outside of town.

We laughed and carried on that night, all of us drinking more than we should. Levi and I kept making eyes at each other but did so in a way that wasn't obvious to everyone else.

It was pretty late in the evening before the crowd from the bonfire party began thinning out. As we made our way to leave, I questioned whether any of us should be driving. The truth is, none of us were sober, but out of the four of us, Troy seemed to be the least drunk. So, him getting behind the wheel seemed to make the most sense. I hopped in the back seat with Levi, and we started making our way home.

We were just a few miles down the road when Troy turned onto Cooper's Farm Road, a mostly secluded road that just about made a straight line through the woods to the edge of town. There were multiple hills along the road, and teenagers like us often made a night out of driving too fast down the road and hill hopping. It was a tradition in our town that had been going on for many generations, and when he took that turn, I knew exactly what he had in mind.

As he raced down the road, accelerating each time we approached a hill, Levi and I slowly crept our hands across the middle of the back seat until they were touching. We kept tapping our fingers against each other's hands while laughing as the car occasionally took flight, its tires leaving the road.

It excited me knowing that we would be spending the night together, just the two of us, and that Troy and Marcus were oblivious to it all. The night seemed to be ending on a high note, and it felt like the best day of my life.

Then, as we crested the final hill and the tires went airborne, I saw lights ahead.

"Shit!" Troy screamed, gripping the wheel in an attempt to keep control once the tires met the pavement.

Sadly, he wasn't able to. The car veered to the left a bit, clipping the front corner of the oncoming car. The other car swerved to avoid impact but lost control on the wet road.

It all seemed to happen in a flash. One moment, it was like we were still in the air, then the next, we were sitting there in shock. We checked to make sure we were okay before stepping out of the car to check on the other driver. There, we saw the other car smashed into the trunk of a large tree.

"Fuck!" I screamed and began running over to the car. The others followed just behind me.

Approaching the driver's side window, I saw a middle-aged man slumped over in the driver's seat. He hadn't been wearing his seatbelt, and it was clear that his head had smashed against the windshield. I knew in my heart that he was gone, but Troy still reached out to check for a pulse.

Troy, being from one of the richest families in our town, was the only one in our group that had a cell phone. He immediately called his dad, and within minutes, both his dad and the town sheriff were standing there on the road with us.

The fact that Troy was our school's football star, along with the fact that his dad was best friends with the Sheriff, was the only thing that saved our asses that night. They talked quietly with each other for a few minutes before Troy's dad approached us.

Looking directly at Troy, he took a stern tone. "What you're going to do is follow me home. You're going to park your car in the garage, and it's going to stay there until we can get that bumper replaced. Your little friends here," he said, gesturing at the rest of us, "are going to go home and not tell anyone what happened here. Is that clear?"

"But what about..." I began.

He raised his hand, gesturing for me to shut up. "You boys have been friends for a long time, yeah?"

We all nodded.

"I don't want my son going down for a stupid mistake, and I'm sure none of you wants to go down with him. Correct?"

No one said a word.

"We can make this go away. You all just have to keep quiet and not run your fucking mouths to anyone. Understood?"

We all nodded again in unison as if we were in boot camp responding to a drill sergeant.

A few days later, I read about the accident in the paper. The man's name was Greg Reeder. The autopsy declared head trauma as his cause of death. The article also stated that the man was driving drunk.

Helen, Greg's wife, was not happy about that fact at all. She was on the news one night, ranting and raving that the police report had to be a lie. She said her husband wasn't a drinker at all, and there was no way the accident had happened the way they said it had.

The people in town showed her sympathy but brushed off any accusations she threw out. The sheriff was a well-respected man in town, and people often took his word at face value. I couldn't help but wonder how many times he had done this for someone.

Troy was like a celebrity in our town, and his status, along with his father's relationship with the sheriff, helped us get away with murder. We did our best to play it cool afterward, but it seemed to be easier for the others than it had been for me. I've always wondered if that's what led to the four of us drifting apart so easily after graduation, just like I've always wondered if that's why I've been so hung up on Levi ever since.

CHAPTER 4

WE SPENT THE REMAINDER of the drive to the airport in awkward silence. It wasn't until we were in line for TSA that Levi finally broke the silence.

"Who hurt you?" he asked quietly as we stood in line.

"Huh?"

"You said someone hurt you. Who was it?"

"It was just Steven, but that's not an issue anymore."

"The uh... one that died?"

"Yeah. That would be him."

"What did he do? Did he hit you?"

"The short answer is yes, but that was usually the easiest to deal with."

"What do you mean?"

"The reality is that he abused me in many ways. Constant yelling and screaming at me as if I were a child, emotional manipulation, gaslighting, accusations of cheating on a regular basis and basically alienating me from everyone in my life. Those things hurt worse and leave bigger scars than someone simply hitting you."

Levi's face took on an angry expression. "He did all that to you? And you let him? I can't believe I went to that fucker's funeral."

I had almost forgotten that had been the last time I had seen Levi before this weekend. To be honest, that whole era of my life just felt like a blur anymore. I remember him being there and offering his condolences, along with his disappointment that I hadn't reached out to him when Steven died. I apologized and told him there was just so much going on that it slipped my mind.

I never mentioned the real reason was that I had spent years wallowing in self-pity and didn't want to bother any of them with my problems, especially since the cause of Steven's death was a car accident, which felt like nothing but a huge reminder of what had happened years before.

I later learned that Levi and the others had apparently all found out about Steven's death through mutual friends. Though Levi was the only one to show up, Marcus and Troy sent along their condolences with him. I appreciated the gesture of him showing up but was cold and distant to him at the time. I was already dealing with the combination of the happiness that Steven was no longer around to abuse me and guilt at the fact that I not only felt such happiness but also that I was doing my best to feign sadness around his family.

I was also dealing with the realization that my isolation from the rest of the world was no more. My prison cell had officially been opened, and after years of being forced to put every ounce of my focus into one person, I would now have to learn to live for myself again.

I had done my best over the past two years to forget that period of my life; to push it away so it just felt like a bad dream, but talking to Levi about it brought every bit of it rushing back.

"I'm sorry you had to deal with that. I wish I had known," Levi said, noticing my emotional state from reliving the memory.

"There was nothing you could have done. It was my prison, and it was up to me to escape. I just wish I had done it on my own."

I wanted so badly to tell him the truth, the part of the story that I had never told anyone else, but kept my mouth shut. I let the silence be a moment of peace as we made our way through the rest of the line.

ONCE WE HAD GOTTEN through TSA, we made our way to our gate to sit and wait for our flight. As we sat there, making small talk, I could see what looked like sympathy in Levi's eyes.

"Please don't do that," I said, interrupting our conversation.

"Do what?"

"Pity me. I can see it in your eyes."

"I just hate that he hurt you like that is all. You've always been good and cared about others. You deserve better than what life has dealt you."

"I'm actually not doing too bad. Things have been slowly getting better since Steven has been gone. It may not seem like it, but they are. It's just... seeing you brought a lot of stuff back."

"Well, if it makes you feel any better, my life hasn't been the picture-perfect scenario you seem to think it is."

This caught me off guard. From all appearances, at least on social media, it seemed like he had everything. He must have noticed my confused look, because he answered the question I hadn't even asked out loud.

"We've kept things quiet, but Erin and I are technically separated. We basically pretend around everyone, including the kids."

"Oh, shit," I said, feeling a mix of both sympathy and excitement. I knew it had to hurt him, but I won't deny that it made me wonder if there was a chance for something more between the two of us.

"Yeah. Kyra is already in college, but Mason just started his senior year. We've agreed to make it official and file for divorce once he's out of school."

"I'm sorry. I... I didn't know."

"It's okay. Things used to be good, but we just grew apart."

I sat there unsure of what to say. "I... uhh..."

"I know what you're thinking," he said, cutting me off, "and seeing you again has me thinking the same thing."

My heart began racing.

"I'm not making any guarantees, and you need to be patient with me, but I'd like us to see each other more often after this weekend. If that's okay with you."

"Um, yeah. Of course."

"I mean it. I'm not sure if this is the path I want, but I also don't want to let the opportunity slip away. It's going to be a long, complicated road. I just need you to understand that. If that's not okay with you, I won't be mad."

"I can do that," I said, trying to hold my balloon of hope at a reasonable height.

I wanted to ask why he hadn't said anything earlier, why he waited until after my little outburst to speak up, but I didn't want to ruin the moment. Instead, we just sat there in silence until it was time to board the plane.

———

OUR SEATS WERE TOWARD the back of the plane. I had the window seat, and Levi was in the middle. I sat there and waited for someone to come down and take the aisle seat, but it never happened. I expected Levi to move over to the aisle seat to have a little more room, but he didn't. He stayed next to me, our legs and arms touching.

Shortly after takeoff, I felt Levi's hand grab mine. It felt as though a wave of comfort washed over me in that moment, and before too long, I dozed off.

At some point, I slipped into a dream state. I was back in my old car, a silver Honda Civic. Rain was pouring down over the car as I drove, and Steven, my ex, was sitting in the passenger seat. I was reliving the night of the crash; the night Steven died.

The range of emotions I felt that night came rushing back. I was doing my best to drive along the highway, despite the limited visibility the rain offered. I was on the verge of a panic attack as Steven sat there in the passenger seat, screaming at me and belittling me for some mundane thing he saw fit to complain about. This had all become a regular occurrence, and I was in a mental state where I felt trapped in my situation, desperate for an escape.

To this day, I'm still not quite sure what happened, or how it happened, but one moment, I was driving, and the next, we crashed into a concrete structure. The car was facing downhill, and rebar had broken through the windshield and penetrated Steven's skull.

His lifeless body sat there beside me, blood pouring from his wounds.

I had had this vivid nightmare, reliving that terrible night, multiple times. However, this time, it ended differently. As I stared at Steven's lifeless body, I saw his eyes shift in my direction, looking right at me.

"Are you just going to leave me here like this?"

The ground below me shook, and I was startled awake. The plane landing had pulled me out of the nightmare.

I sat straight up and gasped.

"Are you okay?" Levi asked, just now pulling his hand away from mine.

"Yeah. Uh... yeah. The landing just startled me."

Chapter 5

IT TOOK UNTIL WE made it down to our luggage carousel before my nerves calmed some and my body stopped shaking.

"Well, shit."

A voice from behind caught us off guard as we watched the carousel begin to move. I turned to see Marcus standing behind us.

"Hey!" Levi called out as he stepped in to give Marcus the stereotypical bro hug that begins with a handshake. I stepped in next and did the same.

"How was the flight?" he asked.

"It was fine."

"I got in about an hour ago. Told Troy I'd wait for you two and let him know when you were here. He should be by to pick us up here in a few."

"Good to see you, Marcus. It's been too long," I said, looking him up and down. Levi may have been the one I was in love with, but Marcus had always been a good-looking guy as well.

"You too, man. Both of you. I'm glad Troy arranged this get-together. It's gonna be a great time."

"Do you know where he's taking us? What this surprise is?" I asked.

"No clue, man, but when I called him, it sounded like he had someone with him."

"I thought this was a guy's trip. No wives," Levi said, sounding annoyed.

Marcus laughed. "No, it wasn't his wife. It was definitely a guy's voice I heard. Probably one of his football buddies or something."

We continued to make small talk as we waited for our bags. Once we had them, we stepped outside to find Troy already waiting for us. He was standing in front of a large Chevy Suburban. We almost didn't recognize him, as he had gone from his usual look of shaggy hair and a clean-shaven face to a military-style flat top and a mustache. He looked like a cop from a 70s porno. Noticing the confused look on our faces, Troy laughed.

"Incognito. My goal is to enjoy the weekend with you boys without being recognized," he said, gesturing towards his face.

The hatch on the back of the Suburban opened, and the three of us placed our bags inside while going through another round of handshakes and bro-hugs. Afterward, we took our seats in the truck; Levi, Marcus, and I in the back seat, and Troy in the front next to his friend.

"Fellas, this is Paul," Troy said.

Paul turned to face us and reached out his hand. He was a good-looking man, blond hair, blue eyes, a few days' worth of stubble forming on his chiseled jawline.

"This one of your football buddies?" Marcus asked.

"No. We actually just met two days ago. He's gonna tag along for our little adventure."

"Football buddies?" Paul asked.

"Yeah," Troy said with a nervous laugh. "I have some local buddies I play some ball with. Just a bunch of dads in the neighborhood who wished they'd gone pro."

Turning to look at the three of us, Troy gave a nervous smile and winked. We all nodded; his message received loud and clear.

"What is this little adventure going to be?" I asked.

"We'll get to that in a bit, but let me tell you, it's something even better now that Paul is tagging along."

He must have noticed the confused look all three of us had, because he laughed and said, "Just trust me."

We pulled into a diner just outside of the city about thirty minutes later. Once we had ordered, Troy went straight to business.

"Okay, so the plan for tonight is to head to the strip club and have some drinks. You know, really unwind and get this trip going."

Paul stood up. "Gotta piss, fellas."

As he stepped away, I looked at Troy. "A strip club?" I asked with a laugh, holding back from rolling my eyes.

"Look, I haven't been to one in forever." He paused, looking to make sure Paul was out of earshot. "Too high-profile. Since I'm in incognito mode for the time being, I'm taking full advantage of it."

"I hope that's not all you have planned," Levi added.

"No, smart ass. It's not," Troy replied. "Originally, my plan was to hit a few of the national park sights in the area, and we still might do that if we have time, but Paul showed me something even cooler."

"What is it?" I asked.

Paul startling us with his sudden return, placed a piece of paper on the table. On it, there was a crudely drawn map. The map had a curvy dotted line, which I assumed to be a trail. Along the trail, there were six Xs, each with locations written beside them: Trailhead, Devil's Hall, Tea Table, Hoodoo Garden, Forest Of Dreams, and Demon Throne.

Marcus, Levi, and I looked over the map, then returned our gaze to Troy and Paul.

"This is the Bryson Badlands. It's very remote, in Indian Territory. Way off the beaten path, but absolutely worth the trip," Paul said.

"What's so special about it?" Marcus asked.

"It's one of the coolest places I've ever seen. It's basically a wash in the middle of the desert, full of amazing rock formations and hoodoos. It's like an acid trip, man. Feels like you've stepped onto another planet," he said. He pulled out his phone and swiped the screen, tapping a few times before handing it over to us.

On the screen, there was a photo of a rock formation resembling a tree. Holding the phone, Levi began to swipe through the photos as Marcus and I watched. Picture after picture of the wildest rock formations I've ever seen. I won't even deny that I was intrigued.

"So, you've been here before?" I asked Paul.

"Yeah. Just before I met your buddy here," he gestured towards Troy. "A friend of mine gave me this map, along with directions on how to get there, before I flew out here for vacation. I was already planning on going back before flying home, but after meeting Troy, I figured I'd just hang with him and help you all find it."

"That's really cool, man. This place looks awesome," Levi said.

"We'll easily spend most of the day there. The map doesn't do justice to how big the place it."

"So, you said this is in Indian Territory. Are we allowed to go there? Isn't stuff like this sacred in their culture?"

"I'm pretty sure that's not an issue," Paul began, pausing for a moment. "Besides, even if it was, it's so far off the beaten path. Nobody would even know we were there. I went by myself, and I'd bet a month's salary that there wasn't another person around for a ten-mile radius."

As we sat and ate our food, I couldn't help but notice how chummy Troy and Paul seemed to be for two guys who had only known each other for a day or two. We were the ones he had been friends with since we were kids, but he seemed more excited about this new friend than he was about seeing us. There was also the fact that, in such a short time, Troy basically hung up the original plans for this trip to go to some place none of us even knew existed. It just made it all the stranger that he had done this while also keeping his celebrity status a secret from him.

The whole thing just seemed off, and something about Paul gave me a weird vibe. It wasn't anything he did or said, necessarily, but just a feeling I got. He seemed almost too friendly. It gave me the impression that he was fake, and it made me wonder if there was an ulterior motive for bringing us out to the badlands.

Chapter 6

THERE WAS ABOUT AN hour of driving after we left the diner before we arrived at our hotel. It was a rundown roadside lodge on the side of the highway. It sat just outside a small desert town called Prosper. I wasn't at all surprised to see the seedy-looking strip club just across the highway, showing that Troy chose location rather than quality when it came to finding lodging for the weekend.

Surprisingly, the rooms weren't as bad as I expected from the outside. They were small, but sufficient and clean. Troy had rented us each a room, as each room only had one bed. I was thankful for this privacy, and also thankful that Levi and I had adjoining rooms. It was safe for me to assume we would be making use of that feature and sleeping together in privacy.

My assumption was quickly proven correct when, after a few moments of being in the room, I heard Levi open the door of his room and knock on my door. Neither of us said a word as I opened it. We made our way over to my bed and lay down together, holding each other and kissing.

Just as our hands were beginning to wander, there was a knock on the outside door. Standing up to answer it, I let out a sigh, frustrated at being interrupted. Levi quickly made his way back to his own room and closed the door before I answered the knock.

I opened the door to see Marcus, Paul, and Troy standing outside. Behind them, the sun had almost completely set.

"You ready to head over to the club?" Troy asked.

I nodded.

"Cool," he replied. "Let's get your boyfriend and head over then."

They all chuckled at the joke. A part of me froze for a moment, wondering if they knew. I realized that they didn't, and it was, in fact, a joke, but Paul seemed to notice my hesitation. The grin on his face after seeing it was one I didn't trust.

Does he know? I wondered. *Did he figure it out?*

I shrugged it off as best as I could and stepped outside to join them. Within a few minutes, Levi joined us, and we were walking across the desert highway.

THE STRIP CLUB WAS about what I expected. A seedy old building with dim lighting that looked as though nothing inside had been updated in decades. There was a dankness to it, like most small-town strip clubs, but surprisingly had a decent crowd.

The playlist for the place also seemed as though it hadn't been updated in decades, playing mostly classic rock and sleazy 80s hair bands. I let out a chuckle as we entered, only to hear Warrant's 'Cherry Pie' blasting from the speakers. I knew I'd be hearing songs like 'Girls Girls Girls', 'Touch Too Much', and 'Slide It In' playing on those speakers before the night was over, and I wasn't wrong.

We each took a seat around the platform where the strippers were dancing, and Troy ordered what would be the first of many rounds of drinks for the night. The waitress stared at Troy for a moment, a hint of recognition in her expression.

"Do I know you? You look awfully familiar."

Playing it off, Troy laughed, "Must be my striking resemblance to Matthew McConaughey."

He wasn't wrong. With his current shaggy appearance, he did kind of look like him. The waitress seemed to agree.

"Well, Mr. McConaughey. Next time you hit our little club here, be sure to bring some of your Magic Mike buddies with you," she replied with a laugh."

"Hey now," Marcus said, playing as though he was offended. "We may not be buff like those dudes, but we could still get some ladies going if we wanted to." He played his statement up even more by pulling up his sleeve and flexing his biceps.

"I'm sure you could, but you'd probably have to lose that wedding ring first," she said.

Marcus blushed, and I saw a twinge of shame come across his face. From the way I had heard him talk about his wife, I could tell he was still very much in love with her. I could tell he had no plans of telling her he had come here, something he already felt guilty about.

As the waitress left to get our drinks, he and I sat quietly for a moment while the others carried on. I reached over and put my arm around him, pulling him a bit closer. I leaned towards his ear. "It's really good to see you, man. I'm glad Troy arranged this trip for all of us."

Distracted from his momentary guilt, he smiled. "You too. It's good to have the whole gang back together again. Feels like old times."

Our drinks came soon after, and I feigned interest in watching the strippers while the others enjoyed their time. I could tell that Levi wasn't super interested in them either. I was pretty sure the one thing we both wanted was to finish what was interrupted when the others knocked on my hotel room door.

THE DRINKS WERE HITTING me fast as the rounds kept coming. At one point, I noticed that Troy had been gone for a while. I looked around the club to see where he had gone but couldn't spot him anywhere. I leaned in toward Levi.

"Where did Troy go?"

He shrugged and began looking around as well. Marcus hadn't seemed to notice, but as Levi and I talked, I noticed Paul looking at me again, with the same grin he had outside of the hotel room. I nodded my head and turned my attention back towards the woman dancing on the stage with her tits out, once again pretending to be interested.

A few minutes later, I was startled by Troy approaching us from behind. He placed his hand on my shoulder and leaned his head between me and Levi. "I come bearing gifts."

In my periphery, I saw his other hand slip something into Levi's shirt pocket.

"Go to the bathroom in the far corner. That one hardly ever gets used."

He made a sniffing sound before standing up and making his way back to his seat. Even in my drunken state, I knew he had slipped some coke into Levi's pocket.

"You wanna?" Levi asked.

I nodded.

"You go first. I'll head over in a minute or so. So, it's not obvious.

I nodded again and stood up to head to the bathroom. Opening the door, I wasn't surprised at the state of the room. A dirty tile floor that had probably been white at some point, a trough urinal that someone had dumped a bunch of ice into, and two toilet stalls in the back. I walked to the rear stall and stepped inside to wait for Levi, doing my best to ignore the strong smell of piss that seemed to permeate every square inch of the room.

It wasn't long before the door opened, and Levi stepped in. He joined me in the stall and closed the door. Pulling the small bag from his pocket, he dumped a small line of coke onto my right hand. I put my left hand up to my nose, holding that nostril shut, and snorted the white powder. I then raised my hand back up for him to dump out a line for himself.

It had been years since I had done coke, and the line hit me fast. My heart began racing, and I felt an intense rush take over my body. I grew an instant erection and was overcome with a sense of lust. I grabbed Levi and pulled him in for a kiss as soon as he had placed the bag back into his pocket.

As we kissed, I began unbuttoning his shirt and running my hands up and down his chest and stomach. They quickly made their way to his pants. I hadn't even fully unbuttoned and unzipped them before his hands were doing the same to my pants. I grabbed his hard cock with my hand and gave it a squeeze before bending over and placing my hands on the back of the toilet.

There was some pain as he first entered me but mixed with pleasure. It felt so good having him inside me. I did my best not to moan loudly as he fucked me, slow at first, but picking up speed as he went on.

I spit in my hand and began stroking my cock as he fucked me, breathing heavily as he did so and losing myself completely in the moment of passion. Before I knew it, he had cum inside me, and before he was finished, I shot my load onto the dirty floor.

I stood up once he pulled out, and we both stood there, basically panting as we got our pants back up. He was still buttoning his shirt back up when we stepped out of the stall to find Paul standing in front of the sink, watching us. He had that same grin again, and I saw Levi's face turn red. I felt as though I had completely sobered up within seconds.

"We... uh..." Levi started, stumbling on his words.

Paul laughed, "It ain't my business what you boys do behind closed doors."

He nodded his head before leaving the restroom. I could see a bit of relief on Levi's face and wished I could feel the same. There was something in Paul's tone, along with that grin. It was something I didn't trust. I worried that he would say something to Marcus and Troy. I wondered how they would react. They weren't homophobes by any means, but they knew Levi was married, and they were all friends with his wife.

A selfish, greedy part of me wanted this to be out, to get it over with so Levi wouldn't have to hide his interest in me, but I also didn't want to see him hurt. He had a long road ahead, one that I had traveled a long time ago. I wanted him to be able to get there at his own pace.

ONCE LEVI AND I got back to our seats around the stage, everything seemed to go back to normal. Marcus didn't seem to notice we had gone anywhere, and Troy just thought we had been doing his coke.

I chugged the remainder of the drink I had left in front of me and quickly ordered another. I wanted my buzz back. I wanted the fun to resume, and for a while, it did.

The five of us continued to drink and carry on for a while. At least until closing time was approaching, and the place began to clear out. Just as the cocktail waitress had taken our final orders for last call, Troy spoke up.

"Who wants a lap dance? I'm paying."

Marcus and Paul raised their hands. Levi and I didn't. My lack of interest didn't surprise Marcus or Troy, but Levi's did.

"You don't want one?" Troy asked.

"I think he's already had his fun for the night. Or has he?" Paul asked, showing that grin again.

Levi stood up. "I think I'm just going to head back to the room. I'm fucking beat from the flight today."

He played it off well, not feeding into Paul's bait. He stood up and began walking to the door.

"Is he okay?" Troy asked.

I shrugged, feigning ignorance. "It has been a long day, with travel and all."

"Maybe you should go check on him," Paul said with a wink. "Go tuck him in and make sure he gets a good night's rest."

I rolled my eyes.

"They're just friends, dude," Troy said. "Jimmy here is the only one that plays for the other team."

"If you say so," Paul said with a chuckle.

I stood up and began heading for the door. Behind me, I could hear Paul call out, "I'm just fucking with you, dude."

I flipped him off from behind before stepping outside and heading back across the highway. Once I was back inside my room, I opened the adjoining door to find Levi's already open. He was sitting on the bed waiting for me.

"You okay?" I asked.

"I'm fine. He just pissed me off."

"Yeah. Something about that dude I don't like."

"Me too, but I don't want to make things awkward for the others."

I nodded.

"I don't know why I'm even letting it bother me. They probably already know anyway."

"Why do you say that?"

"I don't know. I mean, the four of us always hung out together, but they were always closer to each other than they were with us, and we were the same way. I saw the looks they would give us sometimes when we could carry on with each other. I think they've always known something else was there or at least suspected it."

I had noticed that in the past as well, but I didn't tell him that. Instead, I joined him on the bed, sitting behind him and wrapping my arms around him. I could feel his tension relieve some in my arms as we sat there. Grabbing my hand, Levi brought it to his face and kissed it.

"Thanks for always being there for me. I'm sorry it took me so long to realize how I felt, and I'm sorry for the road we have ahead."

"Don't worry about it. We'll get through all this together. At your pace. I'll always be here.

Soon after, we fell asleep in each other's arms.

CHAPTER 7

WE WOKE THE NEXT morning to a knock at the door. Groggy, and with a monster of a headache, I stood up and slipped through the doorway into my own room, closing the door behind me. I grabbed the blanket on my bed and pulled on it in a few different directions to make sure it looked like I had slept in it.

Within seconds, there was a knock on my door as well. I opened it and stepped out to see Marcus standing there. Troy was at Levi's door, but Paul was nowhere to be seen.

"Cool, glad I got you both. That way I don't have to say it twice."

I held my hand up to shield my eyes from the sun. "What is it?"

"We're heading out in about thirty, so shit, shower, take some Tylenol, get some caffeine... whatever you have to do before we go. Gonna get breakfast, then head out to the badlands."

"Fuck," I muttered under my breath.

Marcus gave me a look of agreement.

"I know we're all feeling it this morning," Troy began, "but that's part of the fun. We'll get hydrated, then sweat out the shit from last night. You'll forget all about your hangover by the time we get there."

"How the fuck are you so goddamn chipper?" Levi asked.

"I had a little left of what I gave you last night. If you still have some, I suggest you use it."

We all stood there in silence for a moment before Troy spoke up again, "Alright boys, let's slap this day in the tits!" He clapped his hands and let out a whooping noise before heading back to his room.

I closed my door with a sigh and stepped back into the room. I opened my side of the adjoining door and collapsed on my bed. Levi opened his side soon after and joined me.

"This is gonna be a rough morning," I said with a laugh.

"Yeah. I feel like dogshit, but I do still have some of that coke left."

"Well, I guess we better get moving," I said, standing up.

I stepped over to the single-cup coffee maker in my room and began brewing a cup while Levi went back to his room to get the baggie from his shirt pocket. We shared what was left in the bag and sipped on the coffee while we got our clothes together for the day.

With some stimulants and ibuprofen beginning to course through our systems, we hopped in the shower together, making sure to keep an eye on the time while we were there. Despite being turned on by each other's touch, neither of us had the energy to satisfy our libidos at the time. We wondered how we would have the energy to hike out in the desert.

We agreed to pick up some gallon jugs of water before beginning our hike. Drinking like that the night before was a dumb idea, and we'd regret it if we didn't make some attempt at getting our bodies hydrated before being out in the heat.

THE FIVE OF US arrived at another diner about an hour later. The combination of caffeine and coke at least had me feeling awake, finally, but I still felt very lethargic. I could tell Levi and Marcus felt the same way. I also had a lingering headache, though the ibuprofen had taken the edge off.

Troy and Paul, however, still seemed quite chipper. To the point where you would almost think they hadn't consumed any alcohol the night before. Something about the whole dynamic between the two of them made me uneasy. It was almost as if Paul had some kind of spell on Troy. I hadn't seen Troy in a long time, but I still talked to him here and there through text and social media, and, while more mature, he still mostly seemed to be the same guy he was when we were in high school. But this weekend, something was different.

The mere presence of Paul on this trip just felt intrusive. That, along with his snide remarks the night before, had me to the point where I wanted to just change my flight and head back home. Levi was the only thing that kept me from doing so.

I stayed quiet throughout breakfast. The others made small talk, but Paul and Troy seemed to be carrying most of the conversation. At one point, I saw Levi pick up his phone and type something out. Within seconds, I felt my phone vibrate in my pocket, followed by Levi nudging me with his elbow. I waited a few minutes before checking it, so as not to be too obvious.

What is the deal with those two?

I typed a quick response before putting my phone back in my pocket.

I wish I knew. One of us should try to talk to him... if we can get him away from Paul for 5 minutes.

Agree, Levi replied. *This is so unlike Troy.*

I looked over at Levi and nodded rather than typing another response. He wasn't wrong.

While Troy wasn't necessarily controlling, he was never really the type to be a follower. People always seemed to follow his lead, and it was clear that he loved that. To sit there and watch him just about hang on Paul's every word was strange. It was like he had a spell on him or something.

ONCE WE HAD FINISHED breakfast, we were back on the road. Paul and Troy carried on with each other in the front seat while Marcus, Levi, and I dozed off in the back. We all woke up when Paul pulled off at a gas station on the Indian reservation.

"Wake up, boys. This is the last stop before we get to the trailhead."

I had to piss something awful, so I made a beeline for the restroom. Marcus came in just behind me. As I finished, I went over to the sink to wash my hands and noticed there were no mirrors on the wall. Something about this was odd to me, as mirrors were commonplace in almost all bathrooms. I remembered hearing something a while back that some native cultures viewed mirrors as portals. I figured that was probably the reason why. I shrugged it off and stepped out of the restroom.

Back in the store, I grabbed a few bottles of water and some snacks to take along for the hike. As I stepped outside, I looked over to see Levi talking to Troy. Paul was nowhere to be seen. *He must have gone into the store*, I thought.

I noticed an older Native American man standing by the corner of the store, smoking a cigarette. I approached the man, half to give Levi more time to talk to Troy, and half to ease my own curiosity.

"Excuse me," I said.

The man replied with a nod.

"I wanted to ask you something."

"Go on," he replied.

"The friend we came out here with, he's taking us to the badlands."

The man's eyes went wide.

"He mentioned that it was on reservation territory. While he doesn't seem to care, I wanted to make sure that wouldn't," I paused, trying to think of the right words, "cause any problems. The last thing I want to do is disrespect your people or your culture."

The man shook his head. "Those badlands are nobody's territory."

"What do you mean? I looked at the map."

"That's not what I mean. There's something dark there. Something—"

"What's going on, fellas?" Paul asked, interrupting the man and putting his hand on my shoulder.

"Nothing," I replied. "Just wanted to ask him something."

"I'm your tour guide today, buddy. Direct all questions my way," he said with a plastic grin.

The Native American man had a look of discomfort on his face before heading back into the store. He gave me an odd nod that felt like a warning before stepping through the door.

Paul kept his hand on my shoulder as we walked back to the truck. "You ready for this hike?" he asked. "We'll be there in about thirty minutes."

I swallowed what felt like a lump in my throat and nodded.

Thinking fast, I pulled Paul's hand from my shoulder. "You go ahead, man. I forgot something. Gonna run back inside real quick."

Paul nodded. "Just make it quick. We need to get our asses moving."

I ran back into the store, barely making it past the doorway before looking out the front window. I waited until I saw Paul get in the truck before waving the Native American man over.

"What were you about to say?" I asked.

"Your friend there. He's already been to the Badlands, hasn't he?"

"He's not my friend, but yeah. He says he has, anyway."

"There's an evil in those badlands. An evil that pre-dates humankind."

I gave him a curious look.

"Many stories have been passed down through generations in my family. Stories of the darkness within those badlands, a darkness that attaches itself to people. Your friend has brought some of it back with him. It's probably why he's trying to lure you out there."

"What do you mean?" I asked.

"It's like a sickness," he replied. "A virus. It wants to spread."

I couldn't believe what I was hearing. I knew something was off about Paul, but this was just too outlandish. It just sounded like generations' worth of paranoid superstition.

I was about to reply when I heard a horn honking from the parking lot. I knew it was Paul trying to rush me, so I thanked the man for his time and turned to head back.

I could feel his eyes watching me as I ran back to the truck. I could picture him shaking his head at me, calling me an idiot under his breath.

IT WASN'T UNTIL WE were all back on the road that Paul asked the question I knew was coming.

"So, what were you asking that old man about?"

I felt no need to lie, so I didn't.

"I asked about the badlands. If it was okay for us to go there."

Paul chuckled, "I told you it was cool, man."

"Well, that's not what he said. He said there's something dark there. That it was nobody's territory."

He waved his hand dismissively. "Probably just trying to scare us off. Afraid we'll mess with stuff or spray graffiti on the rocks."

"Yeah," I said, going along with it. "Probably."

I didn't believe in the supernatural, but something about my conversation with that man left me with even more of a knot in my gut.

CHAPTER 8

Once we turned off the main highway, we drove about fifteen miles on a series of dirt and sand roads. As we went, I couldn't help but think how bad they would be after a decent rain. I imagined how much of a nightmare it would be getting stuck out here. The place truly was in the middle of nowhere. There wasn't a single house anywhere in sight.

It felt even more desolate once we pulled up to the trailhead. It was just a small area free of scrub on the side of the road. Looking around, you couldn't even tell the badlands were anywhere nearby. It just looked like desert scrub as far as the eye could see.

We stepped out of the truck and began loading water bottles and snacks into our backpacks.

"I hope you boys are ready. It's going to be a lot of walking, but I promise it'll be worth it."

"This is what I came out here for, man. Adventure!" Troy replied, giving Paul a high five.

Levi and I just gave each other a look. *He does high-fives now?*

"Well. Come on," Paul said, turning and starting down the trail.

Troy and Marcus followed just behind. Levi and I stayed back a little but followed along as well.

"So, what did Troy say?"

"It was so weird, Jimmy. He's almost like a different person. I know you haven't kept in touch with him all that much, but I have. That's not the Troy I know."

"So, he *is* different. I'm not crazy."

"No, man. Any time I tried to ask him something, he either dodged it or gave some vague answer. And he got defensive as soon as I mentioned Paul."

"Fuck," was all I could think of to say.

"That's not even the weirdest part. His responses almost felt robotic, as if they were pre-programmed. It creeped me out." He paused a moment before continuing, "I'm not gonna bring it up again. At least not on this trip. I'll wait until we're all back home and call him. I just want to try to enjoy this trip as best we can."

I nodded in agreement.

THE TRAIL WENT ON for about half a mile before the wash was visible. The edges of the wash looked to be steep rock walls. Up ahead, the trail went downhill into what looked like a hallway carved into the rock. I assumed this was the 'Devil's Hall' I had seen on the map.

Paul stopped at the base of the slope, just where the hall opened up and turned to face us. "This here is the Devil's Hall. No turning back now, fellas."

"Hell yeah!" Troy exclaimed

Marcus let out a laugh. Levi and I just nodded along. We followed as Paul headed into the wash.

I managed to get Marcus away from the others as we walked. I nodded at Levi, gesturing towards Paul and Troy. Thankfully, he picked up on what I was getting at, and he made his way up towards them in an attempt to distract them while I talked to Marcus.

"Can I ask you something, Marcus?" I said.

"What's up?" he replied, not taking his eyes off his phone screen as he continued to take pictures.

"Doesn't something seem off about all of this?"

"This place is wild, man. I've been telling my wife we need to travel more. She'll definitely agree once she sees these pictures. The kids would love this shit too."

"No," I paused. "That's not what I mean."

He stopped walking and finally turned his attention away from his phone. "So, what do you mean, man?"

"I mean, who the fuck is this Paul guy, anyway? And when have you ever known Troy to follow anyone else's lead? He would never derail his plans and let someone else take over like that."

"Man, look around you. This place is unreal. Probably way cooler than what Troy originally planned, and I'm sure he knew that. You're just being paranoid, Jimmy."

"Maybe I am, but I can't shake this weird feeling, man. Levi feels it too. And then there's that Indian dude I talked to outside of the store. He told me something dark lives here. Something evil."

"Dude, he was just trying to scare us off. He knows there's a lot of ignorant assholes that come to places like this and leave trash and graffiti and shit. I can't say I blame him, but you and I both know our group isn't that type."

"Yeah, I get that, but he also said something about Paul. He said he could see something from this place had attached itself to him."

Marcus rolled his eyes. "Look, dude. Don't get me wrong. I love my family, but I rarely get the chance to do anything without them. I've tried to convince my wife and kids to try different places, but they always want to go to the beach for vacation, so that's what we do. This is the first time I've ever gotten to travel somewhere other than a goddamn beach, and I'm loving it. I'm not going to let some dude trying to scare us off get into my head, and you shouldn't either."

I realized I wasn't going to change his mind at all, and I knew that if we continued talking one on one, Paul would get suspicious, so I placated him. "Yeah, you're probably right."

"Dude, just forget about what that old man said, okay. It's just superstition or something. I mean, this is the first time all four of us have been together in a long ass time. Let's just enjoy it, man."

I nodded, and we continued walking.

***

Up ahead, I could see the first of the rock formations. As we got closer, it looked like it was a pillar with a large, flat surface on top. We all stopped and pulled out our phones as we got close to it, each taking a series of pictures from different angles. I was still uneasy about the whole thing, but I couldn't deny that the formation was cool to look at.

"This is the Tea Table. Just a bit further to the Hoodoo Garden," Paul said.

"Those are the weirdly shaped formations, right?" Marcus asked.

"Yes," Paul replied. "Like the ones in Bryce Canyon. You can kinda see them from here."

We all looked off into the distance. He was right; you could vaguely make them out up ahead. As the others continued looking, I turned around to see how far we'd come. I couldn't even see the Devil's Hall from where we stood.

"Damn. How far have we walked?" I asked.

"Not quite a mile. Why?" Paul asked.

"I can't see where we came in."

"Haven't done much hiking in the desert, have you?"

I shook my head.

"This whole hike is like that. Mirages and illusions aren't just something in cartoons. The bright sun and landscape can play tricks on you."

"Yeah," Marcus chimed in. "It was like that when I went to Death Valley. Really threw me off, man. I used one of those trail apps to help me find my way."

"That's why it helps to have a tour guide," Troy said with a cheesy smile, gesturing his head towards Paul. I scoffed at this. You'd think they were the ones who had secretly been fucking.

With the phones put away, we continued along the trail. Soon, we approached the Hoodoo Garden. We immediately had our phones out again with the camera app open. We split up and went in different directions as we explored and took pictures of the hoodoos. Paul watched us as we explored, a smile on his face like a father watching his kids open Christmas gifts.

He wasn't lying, I thought as I explored the various rock formations. The strange-looking rock and sand terrain mixed with formations of varying shapes and sizes really did make it feel as though you had stepped onto another planet. The awe I was feeling took over the sense of dread I had earlier in the day. The sweltering heat and sun beating down on my head couldn't even distract me from how magical this place was.

"Isn't this amazing?"

I turned to see Levi approaching me.

"I've never seen anything like it."

"Paul's pictures didn't do this place justice. It really feels like an acid trip or something."

"I can see why the old man at the store didn't want us to come here. This place is beautiful. I'm surprised people haven't ruined the place with trash and graffiti yet."

Our conversation was cut short by the sound of Paul calling out to us, "You all done taking pictures yet? There's more to see."

We made our way back over to him. Troy was already standing beside him, but Marcus was nowhere to be seen.

"Where's Marcus?" I asked as I approached.

Paul shrugged. Troy brought his hands to his mouth. "Marcus! Let's go!"

It was silent for a moment, and then we heard the scream.

CHAPTER 9

WE ALL JUMPED AT the sound of Marcus screaming and began looking around. He was nowhere to be seen.

"Marcus!" I called out.

"Help!"

It sounded far off. I immediately began running in the direction it had come from. The rock formations that surrounded me were disorienting. Every time I changed direction to avoid one, it felt as though I'd been turned around.

"Marcus!" I called out again, hoping he would respond.

"I've been bit!"

He sounded closer this time. The others were following right behind me.

"We're coming!" Levi screamed.

"Hurry!"

My heart dropped at the sight of Marcus lying on the ground by a large rock formation. I hadn't realized he'd wandered off so far.

"Over here!" I called out to the others as I rushed over to Marcus. "What happened?"

"Snakebite," he said through labored breaths.

"Fuck. Where?"

"Both legs," he said, tears forming in his eyes.

The others were beside me now. We all got down on the ground beside him.

"Try not to move those legs, buddy. It'll just pump the venom through your system faster," Troy said in his most reassuring voice.

"Please tell me you have antivenom in your truck," I said to Paul.

He shook his head. "I don't. Hadn't even considered it."

"Fuck," I muttered, pulling out my phone. "No service. What the fuck are we gonna do?

"I'm fucking done, man. Fucking done," Marcus cried, his fear and panic taking the reins.

"One of us needs to suck out the venom," I said, looking at the others.

"We can take care of that. You two try to call for help. I have a CB radio in the truck. Here," Paul said, pulling keys from his pocket and tossing them to me. I caught them and began looking around.

"Which way is the truck?"

Paul pointed between the two rock formations behind me. "That way. You guys go call for help. We'll start moving him in that direction."

I took off in the direction he had pointed. Levi followed just behind. Not knowing much about snake bites, I had no clue how long Marcus had before the venom took him completely. I hoped that Paul and Troy could help him, at least until Levi and I could get an ambulance out there, but I knew it was a long shot.

My mind raced as Levi and I ran, our legs seeming to move on autopilot, trying to get to the truck as fast as possible. I kept looking around, hoping to see the open area with the tea table appear up ahead, but the rock formations only seemed to become more and more dense. It felt like we were rats in a maze, and the walls were closing in on us.

I finally stopped to catch my breath for a moment and realized Levi was no longer right behind me. I turned in circles, seeing only rock formations around me, though these were different than the ones we had been running through. Their long, thin structures with tops that branched out resembled trees.

"The forest of dreams," I said to myself. "Fuck! Levi! We went the wrong way."

I stood there for a moment, waiting for a response, but there was nothing.

I began walking back in what I thought was the direction I had come from. I called out again, "Levi!", but still heard nothing in response.

"Goddamnit!" I cried out.

How the fuck did we go further down the trail? I wondered. *Did Paul send us this way on purpose?*

I picked up my pace, my breathing growing heavier and heavier. Up ahead, I saw a small opening in the rock trees. "There!" I said out loud. "Levi!"

Before I could register that Levi still hadn't responded, I noticed what looked like a car in the opening up ahead. As I got closer, I recognized the car. It was a silver Honda Civic. Its driver-side door sitting wide open.

I SLOWED MY PACE as I approached the car. My blood ran cold at the sight of someone sitting in the passenger seat. I knew right away who was in that seat. I climbed in the open door and sat down next to my dead husband. He turned to face me, his skin pale and his eyes completely black.

"Well, it's about time," he said. "I've been waiting for fucking ever. We're going to be late."

The venom behind his voice, the condescension I lived with for years, sent my emotions spiraling back to the hell I lived throughout most of our relationship. He always had this way of making me feel like a child who, no matter how hard they tried, could never please their parents.

"I'm sorry," I muttered, a phrase that came from my mouth more times than I'd like to admit.

"Any day now," he said with a frustrated sigh.

I closed the car door, and suddenly, the sunny desert that surrounded me washed away. I was now on a dark road, driving through a rainstorm.

"I swear you can never be ready in time for anything. You know I don't feel good. I wanted to leave an hour ago."

I nodded my head. Tears forming in my eyes.

"And what was with that guy flirting with you? I know you were encouraging that shit. You always do. You never take my feelings into consideration."

I remember that night. The party we had gone to. I had a brief conversation with one of the partygoers, someone neither of us had met before. It wasn't remotely flirty, but that didn't matter. Steven accused me of flirting and cheating on him anytime I gave a moment of my attention to someone other than him.

"Did you get his number so you can fuck him later? I know you want to."

And there it was again. The feeling of the world around me caving in. That feeling of stress and misery that came to a head that night. I took a deep breath and pulled the steering wheel to the right.

The car swerved off the road and downhill, not stopping until it crashed into the side of a building that was under construction. We sat there facing downhill. Poles of rebar had broken through the windshield and sat inches from Steven's face.

"What the fuck was that? I swear you can't drive for shit. I'm surprised you haven't wrecked more cars in your lifetime."

His rant continued, but my ears tuned it out. The sound of his voice became a murmur as I looked over at his seatbelt. I could see the monster behind his eyes, the monster I had dealt with for years. I had felt trapped with this monster for too long and was desperate for an escape. In that moment, as if on reflex, I reached over and hit the button, releasing his seatbelt.

Unable to respond fast enough, Steven's body thrust forward and into the rebar. It pierced through his mouth and right eye. His body twitched for a moment as blood poured out, but eventually, it stopped. The silence of the moment was like a reverie. It was the sound of a prison cell being opened. The weight of the world was finally lifted from my shoulders.

I sat there, enjoying the peace, just like I had the night it happened, but was startled when I heard a laugh coming from beside me. I turned to see his face, still impaired by the rebar, but his left eye was looking directly at me.

"Are you just going to leave me here like this?"

Suddenly, I snapped back to reality. I was sitting on the desert floor, the hot sun beating down on me. I wondered why I had relived that night again. I wondered if it was the badlands that did it. Nothing about the place felt real, but it seemed to know my darkest secret. I gathered myself and stood up, turning to find Levi standing there crying.

"What's wrong?" I asked.

"I got lost and—" he paused, catching his breath, "I saw him."

"Who?" I asked.

"Greg Reeder. The man we ran off the road. Did you see him too?"

"Yeah," I lied, realizing he could see I was shaken up too.

"It was so real. It was like I was reliving that night down to the last vivid detail."

I nodded and pulled him in for a hug. I couldn't help but dwell on the irony that the two darkest secrets of my life involved a car accident. I was so afraid to let anyone know about what I had done to Stephen, yet we had done the same thing years prior. Granted, Troy was the one at the wheel, but we were all involved, and we all walked away, letting people believe the man was drunk.

Levi stepped back from our hug, pulling me back into the situation at hand. "How the fuck do we get out of here?"

"I don't know. I feel like this place is fucking with us."

He nodded in agreement. "Yeah. Have you looked at your phone?"

I shook my head.

"Look at it."

I pulled my phone from my pocket and pushed the button to turn it on. The screen lit up, but the image on it was a jumbled mess. I attempted to swipe it, but it just stayed on the same picture.

"What the fuck?"

"It's this place, Jimmy. Something is wrong here. Marcus is going to die here, and the rest of us are never going to get out."

"Do you think Paul did something to us? Like drugged us or something?"

I already knew the answer. Despite having a hallucination just minutes before, I felt completely lucid. I knew it was something about this place, and I was starting to wonder if Paul had lured us here for a reason. Nothing about this trip felt right. Paul's strange demeanor, Troy acting so differently, the hallucinations, the fact that we felt like we were going in circles. I began to wonder if the plane had crashed and we were in some sort of purgatory.

I wondered if this was my punishment for killing Steven. I had spent the past few years justifying what I had done in my own mind, excusing the act because of his constant abuse, but deep down, there was always a sense of guilt too. I knew there would be some penance down the line.

"So, what do we do?" Levi asked, pulling me from my train of thought.

"I don't know. I guess pick a direction and start walk-ing."

"Agreed."

"Stay beside me this time though, so we don't lose each other again."

He nodded, and we began walking at a fast pace. I took the lead, but kept looking back the whole way, making sure he was still there. I hoped this forest wouldn't trick us with any more memories. We all had our secrets, but I had a few I definitely didn't want Levi to see.

Chapter 10

With our phones not working, it was hard to tell how much time was passing, but it felt like close to an hour before we found our way out of the rock trees and back into the hoodoo garden. The sun was already beginning to set. It took even longer for us to weave our way through those formations before we finally came to an opening and saw the others.

By this point, the sun was just barely peeking over the horizon. Paul and Troy were sitting on the ground with their backs to us. Troy had his head in his hands, and Paul had his hand on his shoulder. Beside them, Marcus lay on the ground, lifeless.

Smoke was coming from where they sat as well, and as we got closer, I could see that they had built a fire. *From what?* I wondered, *there isn't a single tree in sight.* Levi and I began running towards them. They must have heard our footsteps, because they both turned to face us at the same time. They both looked confused.

"How did you get back there? The car is that way," Paul said, pointing in the direction opposite of which we came.

"We ran in the direction you told us to," I replied.

"Clearly you didn't, because you would have made it to the car if you had."

"It's this place," I began. "It got us turned around. I feel like it's playing tricks on us."

Troy stood up. There was anger in his eyes I had never seen before. "Of course you would blame this place. You two have had an issue with Paul since you first met him. You've made it clear that you don't want him here, and you're shitting on this place because of it."

"We got lost, I swear," Levi interjected. "We saw things out there. We saw Greg."

"Oh, I'm sure you saw something alright," Paul scoffed.

Levi immediately went into defense mode. "What the fuck is that supposed to mean?"

"You were probably out there fucking while Marcus lay here dying. Yeah, he's dead now, if you hadn't noticed. Venom doesn't take long. Especially when you're bitten twice. We weren't able to get enough of it out."

"We weren't fucking. We got lost," I said, but nobody seemed to hear me.

Paul turned to Troy. "Yeah, your buddies here. Apparently, they're a real pair of lovebirds. I caught them fucking in the bathroom of the strip club last night. They've probably been fucking this whole time."

Troy turned to Levi with a look of disgust. "You're married, dude. You have a family."

"It's not like that," Levi began, unsure how to finish.

"Then what's it like, Levi? Marcus is dead because you two were off doing God knows what. Your wife and kids are at home, completely unaware that you're out here getting it on with your old high school buddy."

Levi stood there, shame all over his face. This angered me more than it should have.

"Wake the fuck up, Troy. Something is seriously wrong here. You meet this guy, what? Two days ago? And suddenly you're best friends? You're acting completely different; this place keeps changing; and where the fuck did he find wood to build a fire? There isn't a tree in sight."

Neither of them responded. Instead, they charged us and tackled us to the ground. Troy, with his larger frame, held me in place while Paul pulled what looked like thin rope out of his pocket. He proceeded to tie Levi's hands together, turning around immediately after and using another small piece of rope to tie his ankles together. Before standing up, he pulled Levi's phone from his pocket and threw it into the fire.

Once he was done, he ran over to his backpack and grabbed more rope. He made his way over to me and began tying my hands and feet together as well. They rifled through my pockets as well. Troy grabbed my phone and threw it into the fire. Paul grabbed his keys and put them back in his pocket. Once they were finished, they both stood up and looked down at us.

"Troy, go grab my backpack."

Troy nodded and went over to grab Paul's backpack. When he returned, he handed it to him. Paul unzipped it and dug around for a moment before pulling out an old Colt 45 revolver. He held it up with a devilish grin.

"Well, Troy, it's been nice, but I no longer need your assistance."

Whatever spell Paul had over Troy must have disappeared instantly, because the expression on his face quickly switched to one of confusion, then to realization, then to guilt. Troy turned to run, but he was too slow. Paul pulled the trigger, and I saw Troy's body fall to the ground.

The bullet had pierced his throat. Blood spurted from the wound and made a gurgling sound as he struggled for breath. He was choking on it.

"You know, I almost hate using guns. It's too quick. Too clean. Too easy."

He stepped forward and stood over Troy, who still lay there struggling to stay alive. He placed the barrel of the gun below Troy's chin and pulled the trigger. The bullet exited Troy's head through the top of his skull. Bits of skull and brain matter sprayed out onto the ground. His blood pooled on top of the dry terrain.

"Pro linebacker Troy Grishaber found dead in the New Mexico desert. Sounds like a good headline to me. How about you boys?"

He knew he played pro-ball all along, I thought.

"You're gonna pay for that, you sick fuck!" Levi said, in an angry tone I'd never heard him use before.

"Wow!" Paul said, feigning offense. "So aggressive. Surprising to hear something so masculine from a guy who likes taking loads in the ass behind his wife's back."

"Why are you doing this?" I asked, tears blurring my vision.

"So many questions from this one," Paul said, gesturing towards me. "Trust me, you'll get your answers, but they won't do you any good. Tell you what, though. I'll answer one right now. That fire over there... well, you were right. There is something about this place. It has a way of providing for those who serve it."

"Serve it?" I asked.

"Another question? I suppose I'll move that one to the bottom of the list."

He began walking over toward a nearby rock formation. Reaching behind it, he pulled out a duffel bag I hadn't seen before. He unzipped it and turned it over, dumping out pieces of chopped wood.

"Just kidding," he said with a laugh. "This place does have power, but I brought this here before. I knew we'd be here well into nightfall. You have to admit it, though. It does add a nice ambiance, doesn't it?"

"I knew it!" Levi screamed. "I knew you planned this shit."

"Why, yes. Your friend here," he gestured to Troy, "was easy to persuade. Athletes usually are. Must be all those head injuries. Makes it easier to program their mind and control them."

"So, you brought us here to kill us?" I asked.

"Kill? Not so much. More like a sacrifice. I needed four. Marcus here was just a fluke. I'm hoping it counts, though. Definitely made my job a little easier."

"You motherfucker!" Levi screamed.

"I've had enough of your macho bullshit," Paul said, grabbing Levi by the back of the shirt and lifting him slightly off the ground. He began dragging him towards the fire.

"No!" I screamed out. I began flailing around, trying to get my hands untied.

Levi did his best to fight against Paul, but it was all fruitless. Within moments, Paul had his head inches away from the flames. He looked me directly in the eyes. "Say goodbye to your boyfriend."

With that, he pushed Levi's face into the fire and held it against the burning embers. His body flailed as the smell of burning hair and flesh permeated the air around us.

"Please," I begged.

With his hand still gripping Levi's shirt, Paul pulled him from the flames. His face was horribly burnt. The skin and muscle tissue melted away like burning plastic. Some of it dripped off onto the ground. I was horrified at the realization that he was still alive. He was still moving, still breathing.

Paul dropped Levi to the ground and rolled him onto his back. I looked at his disfigured face, horrified at the sight of his mouth opening, as if trying to scream, but the only sound that came out was a loud wheezing. I had never heard a sound like that in my life, and I knew it would haunt me for the rest of my life, however much of a life I had left, anyway.

Walking over to his backpack once more, Paul pulled out a bottle full of clear liquid. From the shape of the bottle, I knew it was either rum or vodka. He held it up in my direction, and I could see that it was Everclear. Winking, he smiled at me and said, "Cheers," before taking a large swig. However, instead of swallowing, he spit it onto Levi's mangled face.

"That'll put some hair on your chest."

Levi began convulsing. The wheezing sound coming from his mouth grew louder as his body flailed around.

"Just fucking die already," Paul said, rolling his eyes. I could hear the frustration in his voice. "This one doesn't know when to let up. Maybe he needs another drink."

Paul stepped on Levi's chest to hold him still and poured the clear liquor into his mouth until it overflowed onto his face. He began to flail around some more, but Paul's weight on his chest kept the upper half of his body still. He began to make choking noises, and the clear liquor splashed out of his mouth as he attempted to gasp for breath.

I wanted to break free of the ropes that held me. I wanted to save him, but save him from what? Even if he survived, would he want to go on like that? Disfigured, afraid to show his face in public. Could I even still love him like that? Could I look at that mangled face, or what was left of it, and still feel the same way?

My body went numb at this train of thought, and I watched as his life slowly seemed to fade away. It wasn't long before his body stopped moving altogether.

MY STOMACH CHURNED AT the realization that Levi was dead; gone from my life forever. I would never get to see him smile again. I would never get to feel his body against mine or wake up to his smile again. I knew I should have felt sympathy for his family as well, but my selfishness wouldn't allow me to. In my mind, he had always been mine.

I rolled to my side and threw up the little bit of food still left in my stomach and began sobbing. I was finally given a glimmer of hope for some kind of future with him, something I had waited for years to have, and Paul ripped it away within seconds. I couldn't even look in that direction. I couldn't bear to see his lifeless body or mangled face, a face I fell in love with over twenty years ago.

I felt helpless, like I just wanted to give up. A part of me wanted to just let Paul kill me and put an end to the pathetic life I've lived up to this point, but a larger part of me wanted revenge. I wanted him to pay for taking Levi and the others away from me.

Still lying on my side, I looked at Paul, who was just standing there, staring down at Levi as if proud of what he'd done. "Why?" I asked.

Paul let out a laugh and sat down in front of the fire. "Nothing like a good campfire story, right? Don't go anywhere. This is a good one."

As he continued talking, I quietly brought my feet as far back as they could go. My hands could just touch them. I felt for the rope that kept my feet tied together and began working on the knot.

"I heard your conversation with the old man outside the store. You've probably already figured out that he wasn't lying. There's a dark force in control of these badlands. Many people have disappeared in an attempt to explore this area. This goes back centuries.

"The natives of the area made many attempts to try to push the dark force away, to get it to leave this land for good, but they were never successful. As a result of that, they all keep their distance and do their best to sway others from coming here.

"I first came here about four years ago with my wife, her father, and our two kids. I stumbled upon this place by accident, pretending to be lost. I was really just pretending to be lost so I could find a desolate place to kill them without witnesses. You see, I found out earlier that year that the kids weren't really mine. My wife had been having an affair the whole time we were together. Her prick of a father was in on the whole thing. I had a successful career, and they were all just using me for my money."

I continued listening to his rambling, pretending to be interested in his story while slowly working on the rope around my feet. He had tied one hell of a knot on it, but I was managing to get it undone. I would probably have had it untied already if I wasn't trying so hard to hide what I was doing. I kept working on it as he continued his story.

"I pulled off the dirt road when I noticed the trail-head up there," he said, pointing behind where he was sitting. "My wife, Carol, was being a total cunt, bitching at me for getting lost. I played it off well, though. I told her this was a surprise I had planned, and as we began heading down the trail, I hoped there was something interesting enough to make it believable. I got lucky in that aspect, as you can see.

"As we began exploring the area, we all got turned around, much like you and your friend did here. We ended up getting separated, and I used that to my advantage.

"I took out Carol first, and goddamn it felt good to watch that lying, conniving cunt bleed out. After that, I went for her father. He was getting up there in years, and the heat was beginning to get to him, so he ended up being the easiest of the bunch to get rid of.

"The kids were last. They had always been ungrateful little shits, and a part of me felt like they knew I wasn't their father all along. Twin fifteen-year-old boys I had tried to shape into men, but they were well on their way to being losers like their real father. Once I took them out, I felt compelled to walk in that direction."

I didn't have to look to know he was pointing towards the forest of dreams.

"If I had realized what the forest of dreams was, that it showed anyone who entered it their biggest, darkest secrets, I'd have let that cunt Carol explore it before killing her." He shrugged, "Live and learn."

"I was face to face with a few demons from my past before finally making it to the demon throne. And let me tell you, that thing is unlike anything you've ever seen before. You'll have to trust me on that one, because you'll never get to see it. Not alive, anyway.

"The force that controls this place lives there, and it connected with me. It spoke to me without saying a word, and we made a deal. It promised to let me leave here, alive and intact, as long as I promised to bring four sacrifices each year."

I pulled again on the knot and felt it loosen some more. My feet were almost free. One more pull, and I knew I'd probably have it. He continued.

"It was pretty easy, to be honest. Just find some ass-hole like your friend Troy, someone more susceptible to mind control."

"Mind control?" I asked.

"Boy, you just don't stop with the goddamn questions, do you?" He scoffed before continuing. "But yes, mind control. You see, there is so much energy and power in this place, and if you agree to help it, it will loan you some of that power. It lets you see into a person's mind, their dreams, fears, and aspirations, and it lets you control them. All you have to do is convince them to go, and the people with them are likely to follow. It was never hard to find a group of hikers, explorers, or thrill seekers to bring here. So, you see, I'm not doing this to be malicious. I'm doing it to keep myself alive. I won't lie, though. I have taken some joy in this, as you've clearly seen."

The last pull did the trick. I felt the rope slip away from my ankles and fall to the ground. My feet were finally free. I just had to figure out a way to distract him, even if just for a brief moment. I tried the first thing that popped into my head. I sat up and looked in his direction, but not at him. I looked behind him. I widened my eyes as if I saw a glimmer of hope coming from that direction.

"What?" he said, turning around.

I shot up in a way I didn't think possible for the shape I was in. I was immediately on my feet, running as quickly as I could into the rock formations and towards the forest of dreams. If I had any chance of losing him, it would be in that place.

Chapter 11

I COULD HEAR HIM screaming from behind as I ran. With my arms tied behind my back, it was tough to keep my balance while dodging the rock formations. I knew he wasn't far behind, and just hoped I could make it to the forest of dreams in time to find a place to hide and work on getting my hands free. Otherwise, I'd have no hope of escape if he caught up to me.

The moonlight coming from the sky above gave just enough light to let me see the ground ahead of me and avoid any trip hazards. I persisted as I made my way through the rocks, ignoring my exhaustion and my labored breathing until I finally made it into the forest of dreams.

The density of the rock formations made it difficult to run in any certain direction, but I knew it would make it easier to throw Paul off my path. I ducked behind a cluster of rocks shaped like trees and hid while trying to catch my breath.

There was a sharp edge on one of the formations, and I leaned my weight against it, working my body up and down in the hopes that it would cut through the rope, or at least weaken it. The jagged edge of the rock scraped at my skin as it began cutting away at the rope. I had to bite my tongue to keep from screaming and did my best to just focus on getting free.

The skin on my hands and arms was raw and bleeding by the time I got free from the rope. It hurt like hell, but still felt good to have the movement in my arms back. I had finally gotten my breathing to settle some as well. I turned to begin running again but froze as the atmosphere around me changed.

Suddenly, the temperature went from hot and dry to cool and damp. I looked ahead to see a two-story house before me, light blue siding, fenced-in yard, and a two-car garage off to the left side. This was Levi's house, and I immediately knew the memory this place had brought me to.

I began walking towards the house, my body no longer in my control, moving on autopilot as I re-lived this memory. It was shortly after Steven's funeral. Levi and his family had gone on vacation. In my state of vulnerability, I felt compelled to drive down and see where he lived, where he had built the family I was so envious of. I sat in my car, steadily drinking from a bottle of tequila until I finally built up the balls to go inside.

As I stepped out of the car, I looked around to make sure nobody was around before entering his yard and making my way to the back of the house. Like a common burglar from an old movie, I punched a pane of glass beside the back door and prayed Levi didn't have a security system set up.

Once I let myself in, I began exploring the place. It was wonderful, and I hated him for it. He had been very successful in his construction business, and his house was the biggest proof of that success. Nice furniture, large rooms, and pictures of their happy family strewn about the walls and surfaces.

In my anger, I began pulling the pictures from the walls. With each one, I'd throw it down onto the floor and stomp on it. I went into the kitchen and pictured his wife standing at the stove, cooking dinner for her loving family. This image enraged me.

I grabbed a cast-iron pan from the rack over the kitchen island and smashed it into the glass-top stove. I screamed as I ran to the dining room and flipped over the family table.

Once I destroyed that room, I made my way into the living room. My bladder was full, felt ready to burst, so I unzipped my pants, pulled out my dick, and pissed all over their expensive couch.

I went back into the kitchen to retrieve the cast-iron pan before heading into Levi's office. From there, I made short work of smashing his computer to bits and scattering all the paperwork from his filing cabinet all around the floor.

By that point, the realization hit me that I had gone way too far, but it didn't stop me. I admired my destruction for a moment before heading upstairs and into their bedroom.

I spotted a hamper in the corner of the room. It was filled with Levi's dirty work shirts. "Bitch couldn't even do your laundry before your trip," I said with a laugh. "I'd have made sure your clothes were clean."

I reached down and grabbed one of the dirty shirts. I held it to my face and briefly felt my heart warm. It smelled like him, a smell I would always immediately recognize.

I lay on the bed and draped his shirt over my face, taking in his scent as I pulled my cock out and began to stroke it. My breathing quickly turned heavy with excitement as I approached climax, and I shot a load all over my stomach imagining him on top of me.

I used his shirt to clean up my mess, tucking it into my pocket afterward and making my way over to his wife's side of the bed. I stood on the mattress and pulled my pants down, squatting as I did so. The liquor I had been drinking over the last few days had taken a toll on my digestive tract, and I released a torrent of liquid shit onto her side of the bed.

The smell that filled the room was awful, so I jumped off the bed, wiped my ass with her pillowcase, and left the room. I reflected on everything I had done and knew it was time to go.

I made it back to my hotel room that night and slept with the shirt I had stolen beside my head on the pillow.

A few days later, I saw a post from Levi on social media, talking about what had happened and how devastated his family was. They were all terrified that whoever had done it would come back. Further updates came from the aftermath on his social media posts, including his getting new locks, cameras, and a security system installed on his house.

What I had done was unforgivable, and I regretted it constantly. He never found out that it was me who had destroyed their belongings, and for that, I was thankful. It was a betrayal I could never be forgiven for, and I would have lost Levi forever if he had found out.

Similar to the previous memory I had lived out in this place, this one didn't end the way it had in real life. I didn't leave the house and go back to my hotel after defecating on their bed. Instead, I walked back down the stairs and wandered around, taking in all the damage I had done. As I made my way from room to room, I froze at the sight of a man from behind standing in the doorway to the garage.

"Man, you really did a number on this place," It was Levi's voice, but I knew it wasn't Levi standing there. Paul turned around to face me, and now it was his voice speaking. "I'm impressed."

"Fuck you!" I felt the anger from that night come rushing back, only this time, I directed it at Paul.

He opened his mouth to respond to me, but before he could get a word out, I charged at him. I took a jump on my last step, and as my body collided with his, we both went to the ground. The atmosphere around us went hot and dry again, and as I brought my hands to his throat, I saw that we were back in the forest of dreams, no longer in Levi's house.

He smiled at me, taunting me as I attempted to choke him. Despite his face turning red and his strained voice, he seemed unbothered by the pressure I was putting on his windpipe. Behind me, I felt his legs lift. I turned to look and see what he was doing, but it was too late. He had used the weight of his legs to push himself up. His body bucked underneath me, knocking me off. I landed on the ground beside him.

He was on top of me now and rolled me to my stomach. I heard the sound of something metal hitting the ground, followed by his pants being unbuckled.

"Maybe I'll give you one last fuck before you go, since your boyfriend isn't around to do it anymore. Maybe when I'm done, you can tell me who's better."

He let out a maniacal laugh. I felt his weight lift off of me for a moment, followed by his hand grabbing the back of my pants. I took a chance and reached back as he attempted to pull my pants down and hit my intended target. I grabbed his limp dick and pulled, twisting as I did so.

I felt his weight lift off of me and, not letting go of his penis, pushed myself so I was up on my knees. Turning my body, I saw it was a knife he had dropped to the ground when he had unbuckled his pants. I grabbed the knife, and with a quick swipe, I removed his manhood. He fell to the ground screaming, landing on his back.

I moved over to him quickly and shoved the knife between his legs. Between the scream that followed, along with the fact that he turned his head and vomited, I knew I had penetrated his balls. I climbed on top of him and straddled his body. He fought beneath my weight, but he was in a weakened state. Whatever power he had spoken of that was given to him was waning. A balance was being thrown off.

Lifting the knife up, I brought it down, dead center of his chest with all the force I could muster. He grunted in pain and had a look of shock in his eyes. He hadn't expected this wrench I had thrown in his plans. He had expected to walk away completely unharmed. He was probably already planning his return the following year to bring more innocent people to their deaths for some mysterious being.

I lifted the knife and brought it back down again, slightly to the left of the hole from my first stab. I repeated this action over and over again. Blood poured from the wounds, and I heard the sound of bones cracking with each penetration of the knife. I continued this for a while, even after his body had stopped moving.

Then, I heard it. The sound he had described to me earlier when he was telling me his story. The low-pitched hum of a trumpet. The sound seemed as though it was coming from all around me. It was almost deafening, and I cowered to the ground, covering my ears.

As soon as it finished, the ground beneath me began to shake. Dust from the dried dirt and sand below me kicked up, looking like smoke as it filled the air from the earth's shaking. It was choking me, and I pulled my shirt up over my mouth to keep from breathing any more in.

From that moment, I felt compelled to stand up. I had the urge to start walking again. I knew I needed to listen to whatever it was that was guiding me, so I stood up and began moving, and just like Paul said, it was like I already knew which direction to go. I no longer felt lost in this place.

I made my way through the forest of dreams until it opened onto a large clearing. It didn't take very long to reach the end, because I was no longer being turned around by distractions. Up ahead, there was a large rock formation, much bigger than the others I had seen so far. Its odd shape resembled a throne.

Paul hadn't lied to me. It really was a sight to see. It alone was worthy of being considered sacred, not to mention the immense power I could feel coming from within it.

The ground below me rumbled again, and I felt the presence of something else there with me. I couldn't see it, but I knew it was there. I could tell it wasn't from this world. It was something older, something that went beyond what any scientific research could explain. I dropped to my knees in obedience, knowing I was insignificant in comparison to whatever this was.

It began speaking to me without using words. I could feel it inside my head, communicating with me in a way I had never experienced. There was power behind its voice, and I knew it wasn't something I could trick or persuade. I would have to do whatever it told me to do.

What it gave me was a choice to make. An ultimatum. And once I had made my decision, I felt affirmation, and then everything around me went dark.

Epilogue

I'm not sure how much time had gone by after I passed out, but I woke up on the ground just beside the highway we had turned onto to get to the badlands. Standing up, I brushed myself off and began walking until I found someone nice enough to pick me up and give me a ride into town. I must have been in pretty bad shape, because the man insisted on taking me to the hospital. It took some convincing, but by the time we made it into town, I had talked him into dropping me off at the police station.

All it took was saying the name Troy Grishaber for them to take me seriously. Before I knew it, I was sitting in this room, waiting for the detectives to show up.

I ended up waiting for what felt like hours before they finally came in. It was two men. The one looked like a rookie, probably fresh out of training. His young face and clean features looked too polished for him to have been very experienced in his field. The other looked to be about my age. Hints of gray showing in his hair, and wrinkles, probably from years of late nights, paired with a lot of coffee and cigarettes.

As expected, their questions mostly showed concern about Troy's whereabouts, the famous pro football player taking drastic importance over the two family men. I told them my story, as much of it as I wanted to tell them, anyway. I left out some key details so as to not incriminate myself, but I could tell they weren't fully convinced.

I did seem to lose some credibility by not having much information about Paul. I really only had his first name to go by, along with the description and his story about killing his family. They had a team researching the information I provided, but I think we all knew he was probably using a fake name.

They grilled me for a long time, accusing me of being the one to murder my friends and trying to hide it. The fact that I wouldn't tell them where the badlands were located didn't help this assumption. The truth was, I couldn't tell them. It wasn't something I could point out on a map or give GPS coordinates for. I would have to go along and go by sight. I knew deep down that I could find it that way.

This wasn't my only reason, though. I needed to go along with them because I needed to be there to offer them to the entity from the demon throne. I needed to fulfill my end of the deal.

You see, the choice I was given when the entity spoke to me was pretty cut and dry. It had gotten its four sacrifices, but only one of them had been mine. It gave me the option of dying there at the throne and spending an eternity suffering on another plane, or of bringing more back as soon as possible in exchange for my life.

I hadn't done anything meaningful in my life to that point anyway, and with Levi now gone as well. I figured if this entity was willing to bargain with me to let me continue to live, maybe it could bargain with me to bring Levi back as well. It had the power to take him away from me, so surely it had the power to bring him back to me. So, I chose the latter.

I spent my time working on the two detectives, convincing them to bring me with them so they could not only recover the bodies but also investigate what really happened. To my surprise, it was the older of the two detectives that was more susceptible to my persuasion.

I didn't expect to be able to get into the head of the seasoned veteran so easily, but I guess the years on the job had worn him down. The little bit I was able to see inside his mind showed me that he was tired and ready to move on to something less taxing. I could see that he had dreams of moving to the country and opening his own general store with his savings. He would never get to live out that dream, not if I was successful in my mission.

SO HERE I AM, still in this room, waiting for them to get a team together. I wonder how many people they'll bring. I wonder if I'll have to sacrifice them all, or just the three I owe the entity, to make up my end of the deal. And if that's the case, what will happen to the others? If I offer up more, will I be able to get Levi back?

There's only one way to find out, and hopefully, it won't be too much longer. What's important is that we *are* going back to the badlands. There *will* be more bloodshed. I *had* made a bargain after all.

Jason Nickey

Jason Nickey is a horror writer from Charleston, West Virginia. He works mostly in short fiction ranging from quiet horror to extreme. He is best known for his extreme novella, Rural Decay, and his psychological novella, Wreckage. A lifelong fan of all things horror, he can sometimes be found either cosplaying as Jason Voorhees or brushing his luscious beard.

Afterword

The following photos were taken at the Ah-Shi-Sle-Pah Wilderness in San Juan County, New Mexico. I visited this location in August of 2024, and it was a huge inspiration for this story. The landscape is surreal to experience and feels as though you're walking on an alien planet.

As I explored the area, I knew I had to write a story about it. It's pretty far off the beaten path, but if you ever find yourself in New Mexico, I promise it's worth the trouble.

San Juan County, New Mexico

San Juan County, New Mexico

San Juan County, New Mexico

Photos below belong to the author.

ALSO BY UNCOMFORTABLY DARK HORROR

ANTHOLOGIES

Uncomfortably Dark presents The Baker's Dozen-2021 Dark Dozen anthology & the 2022 Splatterpunk award-winning extreme horror anthology.

Uncomfortably Dark presents Trapped-2022 Dark Dozen anthology that explores themes of horror focused on being trapped in an unspeakable situation.

Uncomfortably Dark presents Dark Disasters-2023 Dark Dozen anthology that explores horrific situations unfolding during natural disasters.

Uncomfortably Dark presents Full Throttle-2025 Dark Dozen Anthology that is a full-blown extreme horror anthology dedicated to survivors of sexual violence. *This anthology contains no scenes of sexual violence.*

The Generator-quad collaboration anthology featuring Candace Nola, Eric Butler, M Ennenbach, and Nikolas P. Robinson.

Dark Disturbances- 2024 Uncomfortably Dark Author Sampler Anthology.

Dark Asylum – 2025 Uncomfortably Dark Author Sampler Anthology.
At Midnight, They Feast – 2025 Mini-Halloween Anthology featuring Cassandra Celia, Candace Nola, and Cat Delani

---

NOVELS & COLLECTIONS
EPISODES OF VIOLENCE by David Bernstein
DREAMWHISPERS by M Ennenbach
CREMATED REMAINS by M Ennenbach
CUCKOO by M Ennenbach
OLD TOO SOON by Brian Bowyer
BLACKOUT: MICROPOETRY by Brian Bowyer
INNOCENCE ENDS by Nikolas P. Robinson
HAVE A BLAST by Nikolas P. Robinson
COME OUT & PLAY by Patrick Tumblety
ROADS TO RUIN by Brian Bowyer
SUBJECT A by M Ennenbach
OIOS LYKOS by M Ennenbach
STORYSLAVE by Brian Bowyer
VERUM MALUM by Michael R. Collins
PENNYROYAL TEA by Aaron Lebold
THE SHERIFF OF SALEM by Aaron Lebold
GENOCIDE by Aaron Lebold
QUARANTINE by Aaron Lebold
BLASPHEMY by Aaron Lebold
SLENDER BONES IN SACRED SOIL by Fredrick Niles
THIS IS HOW A VILLAIN IS MADE by Amanda Headlee
COFFEE SHOP by Aaron Lebold

ONE FRIGHT ONLY by Patrick Tumblety
WHITE FLIGHT by Peter O'Keefe

**Order signed copies and limited-edition hardcovers from the shop:
https://www.uncomfortablydark.com/shop**

Join our Patreon for free books, merch, and more!
https://www.patreon.com/user/membership?u=1223133
0&view_as=patron